MEET YASMIN!

written by
SAADIA FARUQI

illustrated by
HATEM ALY

PICTURE WINDOW BOOKS
a capstone imprint

To Mariam for inspiring me, and
Mubashir for helping me find the right
words —S.F.

To my sister, Eman, and her amazing
girls, Jana and Kenzi —H.A.

Meet Yasmin! is published by Picture Window Books,
a Capstone Imprint
1710 Roe Crest Drive
North Mankato, Minnesota 56003
www.mycapstone.com

Text © 2019 Saadia Faruqi
Illustrations © 2019 Picture Window Books

Library of Congress Cataloging-in-Publication Data Names: Faruqi, Saadia,
author. | Aly, Hatem, illustrator. Title: Meet Yasmin! / by Saadia Faruqi ; illustrated
by Hatem Aly. Description: North Mankato, Minnesota : Picture Window Books,
[2018] | Series: Yasmin | Summary: In this compilation of four separately published
books, Pakistani American second grader Yasmin learns to cope with the small
problems of school and home, while gaining confidence in her own skills and
creative abilities. Identifiers: LCCN 2017060828 (print) | LCCN 2017061753 (ebook)
| ISBN 9781684360239 (reflowable ePub) | ISBN 9781684360246 (ebook PDF) |
ISBN 9781684360703 (reflowable mobi) | ISBN 9781684360222 (pbk.) Subjects:
LCSH: Muslim girls--Juvenile fiction. | Muslim families--Juvenile fiction. | Pakistani
Americans--Juvenile fiction. | Creative ability--Juvenile fiction. | Self-confidence-
-Juvenile fiction. | Elementary schools--Juvenile fiction. | CYAC: Creative ability-
-Fiction. | Self-confidence--Fiction. | Schools--Fiction. | Muslims--United States--
Fiction. | Pakistani Americans--Fiction. Classification: LCC PZ7.1.F373 (ebook) | LCC
PZ7.1.F373 Me 2018 (print) | DDC [E]--dc23 LC record available at https://lccn.loc.
gov/2017060828

Editor: Kristen Mohn
Designer: Aruna Rangarajan

Design Elements:
Shutterstock: Art and Fashion, rangsan paidaen

TABLE OF CONTENTS

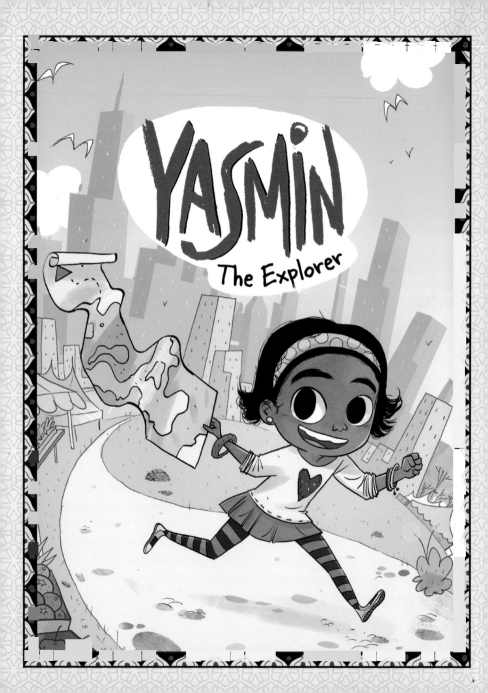

CHAPTER 1

Ancient Maps

One afternoon Yasmin sat reading with Baba.

"A long time ago, explorers used big paper maps to find their way," Baba said.

"What's an explorer?" asked Yasmin.

"Someone who discovers new places. An adventurer," Baba said.

Yasmin looked at the maps in Baba's book. There were straight roads and curvy roads. There were lakes and rivers and forests.

"I want to be an explorer!" she said.

"Well, then, the first thing you'll need is a map," Baba replied.

Yasmin clapped her hands. "I'll make a map of our neighborhood."

"Good idea," Baba said.

Yasmin found
crayons and paper.
She drew their house.
Down the street was
the market. Near that
was the park.

"This is excellent, jaan!" Baba
said, using his sweet name for her.

Soon Mama came in. "Yasmin, I'm going to the farmer's market. Want to come with me?"

Yasmin jumped up. "Yes! It will be an exploration!" She could hardly wait as Mama got her hijab and purse.

"Don't forget your map!" Baba
said. "Every explorer needs a map."

≷ CHAPTER 2 ≷

The Farmer's Market

Mama and Yasmin walked down the street to the farmer's market. The air was fresh and smelled like flowers.

"This way to the market, Mama!" Yasmin said, pointing at her map.

The street was crowded.

There were people
everywhere!

"Hold my hand,
Yasmin. I don't want
you to get lost,"
Mama warned.

Their first stop
was the fruit seller.
Mama bought
strawberries and
bananas. Yasmin sat
down on the sidewalk
and added the fruit
seller to her map.

Their next stop was the bakery stall. It had all sorts of breads, and they all smelled delicious!

Thin ones and fat ones. Big ones and small ones. Yum!

"Two naan, please!" Mama called out.

Yasmin added the bakery stall to her map.

There were so many good smells and things to see. Yasmin saw a man holding balloons. Down the street a lady was selling roses. An ice-cream truck was parked at the corner. Finally, she found what she was looking for.

The playground! Yasmin was itching to explore.

"Mama, the park! I'll be right back!"

CHAPTER 3

A Map to the Rescue

Yasmin ran over to the swings. Swings were her favorite!

Up, up, up!

Then she headed to the sandbox. She would dig for buried treasure!

Yasmin was having so much fun pretending.

Then she thought of something. Where was Mama?

Yasmin looked around, but there were too many kids.

Uh-oh.

Yasmin took a deep breath. "I'm a brave explorer," she reminded herself. "I can find my way back to Mama."

She still had her map. She unrolled it and studied it.

She looked toward the man
with the balloons. Then the
lady selling roses, and the
ice-cream truck. She
saw the fruit seller
where Mama bought
strawberries. And she saw
the bakery stall where Mama
bought the naan.

But no Mama.

Yasmin told herself not to
cry. Explorers don't cry.

Then she saw Mama's blue hijab. She ran toward her. "Mama!"

"There you are, Yasmin!" Mama said. "I was looking for you! You must tell me where you're going!"

"I did, but you didn't hear me. I'm sorry," Yasmin said, crying in relief.

"Let's go home and make dinner," Mama said and hugged Yasmin close. "Baba will be waiting for us."

Yasmin nodded. Next time she went exploring, she would take her map *and* Mama!

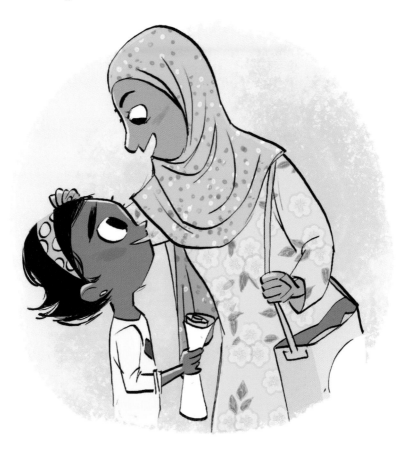

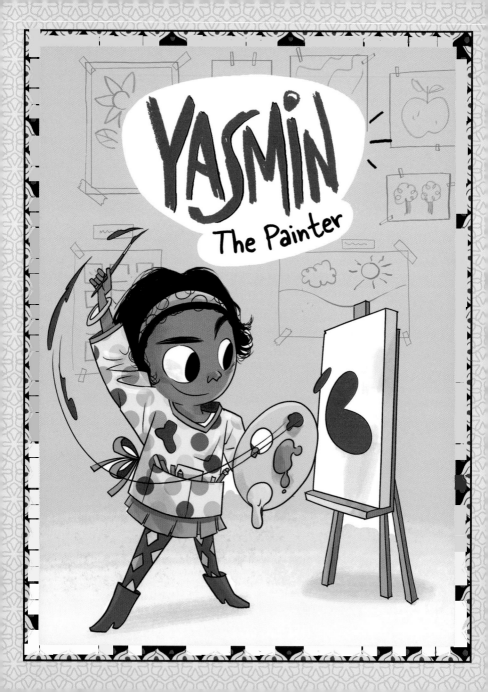

⇒ CHAPTER 1 ⇐

The Announcement

On Monday in art class, Ms. Alex made an announcement.

"We're having an art competition on Friday night! I hope you all enter. The winner will get a special prize."

Everyone was really excited.
Everyone but Yasmin. Yasmin
was worried.

She wasn't very good at art. Her circles were always lopsided.

And her hearts never looked like hearts at all.

"What's the prize?" Ali asked.

"That's a surprise," Ms. Alex replied.

Yasmin frowned.

On Tuesday evening Baba came home with a box. "Yasmin, I have a present for you!" he called.

Yasmin ran downstairs. What was it? A new puzzle? A craft kit?

Baba helped her open the box.

"Oh," said Yasmin. "Paints."

"Yes, for the art competition on Friday. Look, there's an easel, and canvas too!" Baba said.

Yasmin wrinkled her nose. But she said, "Thank you, Baba," and took the supplies upstairs.

⇌ CHAPTER 2 ⇌

Yasmin Makes a Mess

On Wednesday after school, Mama showed Yasmin videos of famous artists. There was a man with a bow tie painting trees. There was an old woman painting mountains.

Yasmin thought of her own messy, ugly artwork. She sighed.

"I'll never be as good as they are."

Mama smiled. "It's OK, jaan. You only have to try your best."

But Yasmin still wasn't ready to paint.

On Thursday Mama said, "Yasmin, finish your schoolwork while I make dinner."

Yasmin watched the video of the man with the bow tie again. He made it look so easy. She decided to give it a try.

She set up the easel and paints and tried to copy him.

A tree was easy,
wasn't it? No.

Maybe a little
flower? No.

Her pictures looked nothing
like the ones on the video.
Yasmin stomped her foot in
frustration.

Oops! Everything scattered
around her.
What a mess!

Then she noticed something. Yellow paint had splotched on the top part of her canvas. She thought it looked like the sun.

She took some brown paint and splashed it on the canvas too.

Then she splashed some blue paint.

Then some green paint.

Soon Yasmin's idea was taking shape.

⇃ CHAPTER 3 ⇂

Competition Day

On Friday night Mama and
Baba walked with Yasmin to
her school. It was weird—and
exciting!—to go to school at night.

Ms. Alex had decorated the
cafeteria with balloons. "Welcome,
children!" she said brightly.

"I can't wait to see what you've created!"

Yasmin had a strange feeling in her tummy, like a hundred soda pop bubbles.

Principal Nguyen was the judge.
He looked at Ali's mountains and
Emma's basketball. He carefully
studied each student's work.

Yasmin pretended to drink her punch. Mama squeezed her shoulder. "Don't worry, your painting is beautiful!"

Soon Mr. Nguyen tapped the microphone. "The winner of the competition is . . . Yasmin Ahmad!"

Yasmin couldn't believe it. Her splotchy meadow painting had won!

But wait—what was the mystery prize?

A man entered the cafeteria. It was the painter from the videos!

"Yasmin, so nice to meet you!" he said. "For your prize I'll be giving you painting lessons next week."

"I have to warn you, I'll probably make a mess!" Yasmin replied.

He laughed. "Don't worry, I will too!"

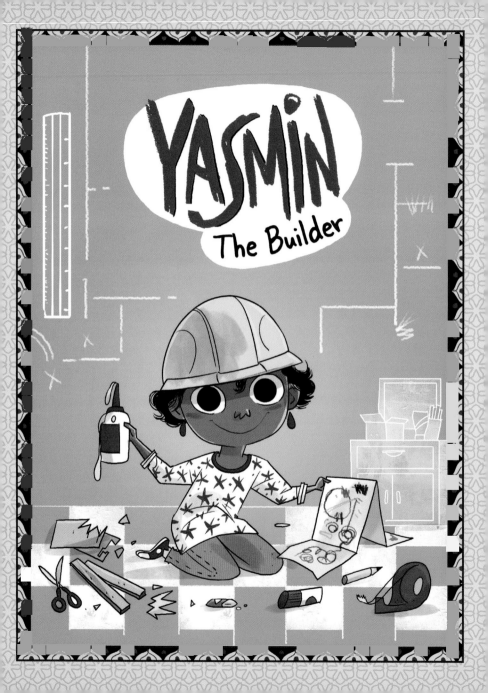

CHAPTER 1

A New Project

Ms. Alex walked into class with a big box.

"We are going to build a city today!" she announced.

The students were very curious. They all crowded around Ms. Alex as she opened the box.

There were tubes and tape,
long sticks and round wheels.

There were connector
circles in bright colors.
Red, blue, yellow, and
green.

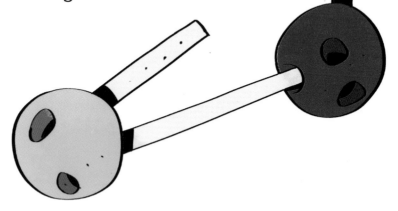

Yasmin watched as Ms. Alex spread the building parts all over the reading rug.

"When can we start?" Ali asked. He reached for a long stick.

"Not yet," replied Ms. Alex. "First you will draw your idea on paper. That way you'll know what supplies you will need."

"Boring!" said Ali.

Yasmin slowly pulled a paper from her desk. She doodled. She sketched. She sighed.

How would these pieces on the floor turn into a city? She didn't know what to make. A roller coaster? An apartment? A zoo?

⇶ CHAPTER 2 ⇷

Get Ready to Build

Finally, Ms. Alex told the students to begin their buildings. "Think of everything a city has," she said. "Be creative!"

Ali was quick. In a few minutes, he built a castle.

"A castle in a city! I wish I'd thought of that," Yasmin said.

Emma was slower. Her church was very tall and had a pointy steeple. "Now I need to make some people," Emma said.

Yasmin sat in the corner,
watching the others. She chewed
her lip. This was harder than
she'd thought.

"Yasmin, why aren't you building something?" Ms. Alex asked.

"All the good ideas are already taken," Yasmin said.

"Well, what do you like to do best in the city?" Ms. Alex replied.

Yasmin shrugged. "I like to take walks. But you don't need to build anything for that."

Slowly Yasmin joined two long sticks together. Then two more. She had no idea what she was making. At least she looked busy.

CRASH!

Yasmin's stick tower fell down into a pile. She hid her face in her hands. What a mess.

⇟ CHAPTER 3 ⇞

Connecting the Dots

Soon, the bell rang for recess.

"We can finish after we get back," said Ms. Alex.

The students left, but Yasmin stayed behind. In the quiet room, she stared at the buildings. There was Ali's castle and Emma's church.

There was a school and three houses. A tall building that looked like a hotel. A grocery store and a gas station and a movie theater.

And Yasmin's messy heap.

She could hear kids playing outside.

"We may go for a walk this afternoon," she heard Ms. Alex call out.

That gave Yasmin an idea. She got to work, collecting all the leftover blocks and sticks and cardboard. She joined them together, here and there.

The recess bell rang just as she finished. Everyone came back in.

Ms. Alex was surprised.

"Yasmin, what's this?"

Yasmin smiled proudly. "The buildings were lonely. I joined them together with sidewalks and bridges."

"Now the people can take walks and visit each other!"

"Wonderful idea, Yasmin," said Ms. Alex.

Emma said, "Hurray for Yasmin the bridge builder!"

≳ CHAPTER 1 ≲

The Closet

Yasmin was bored. Really, really bored.

"When will Mama and Baba come home?" she asked her grandparents. "I'm tired of doing crafts. I already made three bracelets and a crown."

Nani looked up from her sewing. "They just left, Yasmin. Be patient. Surely they can have one evening out at a nice restaurant?"

Yasmin scowled. "They promised to bring me dessert. They better not forget!"

Nana held up his book.

"Come, do you want to read some
of this story with me?"

"No thanks." Yasmin shuffled
away.

She wandered into Mama and Baba's room. Something shiny caught her eye.

Yasmin crept into the huge closet. Brightly colored clothes hung from the rack. Satin kameez, silky hijabs, and beaded saris.

It was like a rainbow
swirling around the room!

CHAPTER 2

An Accident

Yasmin couldn't help herself. She had to try on a new kameez she saw. She twirled around, arms held out, eyes closed.

"What's going on here?" Nani called out.

Yasmin looked up in surprise.

"Nani, these would look good on you!" She looped a hijab on Nani's head. She wrapped a shawl around her shoulders. "Now we're both fashionistas!"

Nani smiled. "I do look nice, don't I?"

The giggles grew louder, and the twirls grew faster, until—OOPS!

Nani stumbled. She stepped on the kameez Yasmin was wearing. Oh no! It was ripped!

Yasmin wailed, "What am I going to do?"

Yasmin took off the kameez. Nani looked at the tear. "Don't worry. I'll tell your mama about it. All will be fine," she said. "I can fix it with my sewing machine."

But the fabric was too thick. It broke the needle on the sewing machine.

"I can fix the machine," Nana said. "Just as soon as I find my glasses . . . "

⚡ CHAPTER 3 ⚡

On the Red Carpet

Nana and Nani were busy
fixing the sewing machine. Mama
and Baba would be home soon.
Yasmin didn't know what to do.

She put on her pajamas.
She tidied up her craft table.
Then she got an idea.

"I know how to fix the kameez!" Yasmin shouted. She held up her glue gun.

Nana tried the glue gun, and presto—it worked!

Then Yasmin had another idea. She took out the feathers and pom-poms and fabric pieces from her craft box. She cut and trimmed and taped them all onto her pajamas.

Now it was as brilliant and colorful as a peacock's tail. Just like Mama's kameez.

They heard Baba's car outside.

"They're here!" Yasmin squealed. "Let's surprise them!"

When Mama and Baba entered, the room was quiet and dark. Then Nana flicked a switch. Lights! Music!

"Welcome to Yasmin's fashion show!" he boomed. "Please prepare for our fashionistas to wow you!"

Yasmin entered and struck a pose. Her pajamas shimmered. Her bangles tinkled. Then Nani joined her, modeling a colorful hijab.

Yasmin and Nani paraded
up and down the carpet, making
sure not to fall. Nani waved like a
queen.

Mama clapped her hands to the
music. Nana took pictures. Baba
yelled, "Amazing! Amazing!"

Yasmin smiled and bowed.
Then she fell onto the couch
between Mama and Baba. "Phew!
I'm starving!" she said. "Did you
bring me some dessert?"

Think About It, Talk About It

* Getting lost can be very scary. Think about what you would do if you got lost. Talk with your family and come up with a plan.

* Yasmin doesn't think she's a very good artist. Why does she feel that way? If Yasmin were your friend, what would you say to her?

* Yasmin has trouble coming up with an idea for the city her class is building. How do you come up with new ideas? What would you add to the city project if you could?

* Yasmin plays dress-up with her nani. What games or activities do you like to do with your relatives?

Learn Urdu with Yasmin!

Yasmin's family speaks both English and Urdu. Urdu is a language from Pakistan. Maybe you already know some Urdu words!

baba (BAH-bah)—father

hijab (HEE-jahb)—scarf covering the hair

jaan (jahn)—life; a sweet nickname for a loved one

kameez (kuh-MEEZ)—long tunic or shirt

mama (MAH-mah)—mother

naan (nahn)—flatbread baked in the oven

nana (NAH-nah)—grandfather on mother's side

nani (NAH-nee)—grandmother on mother's side

sari (SAHR-ee)—dress worn by women in South Asia

Pakistan Facts

Yasmin and her family are proud of their Pakistani culture. Yasmin loves to share facts about Pakistan!

Location

Pakistan is on the continent of Asia, with India on one side and Afghanistan on the other.

Islamabad

PAKISTAN

Currency

The currency, or money, of Pakistan is called the rupee.

Language

The national language of Pakistan is Urdu, but English and several other languages are also spoken there.

سلام

(Salaam means Peace)

History

Independence Day in Pakistan is celebrated on August 14.

MANGO LASSI (YOGURT DRINK)

Ingredients:
- a few ice cubes
- 1 cup (240 ml) plain yogurt
- ½ cup (120 ml) water
- 2 teaspoons (8 g) sugar
- ½ cup (120 ml) canned mango pulp

Directions:
Crush the ice cubes in a blender. Add yogurt, water, sugar, and mango. Blend for about one minute. Serve cold. Yum!

Make a Flower Motif Bookmark

Supplies:

- white cardstock
- scissors
- ruler
- pencil
- colored pencils

Steps:

1. Use ruler and pencil to measure a rectangle bookmark on your paper 2 inches (5 cm) wide and 6 inches (15 cm) long. Cut out the bookmark.

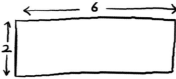

2. On a separate piece of paper, practice drawing the flower in simple steps as shown.

3. Draw three or four of the flower designs on your bookmark, depending on the size of your drawing.

4. Have fun coloring your bookmark!

About the Author

Saadia Faruqi is a Pakistani American writer, interfaith activist, and cultural sensitivity trainer previously profiled in *O Magazine*. She is author of the adult short-story collection, *Brick Walls: Tales of Hope & Courage from Pakistan*. Her essays have been published in *Huffington Post*, *Upworthy*, and *NBC Asian America*. She resides in Houston, Texas, with her husband and children.

About the Illustrator

Hatem Aly is an Egyptian-born illustrator whose work has been featured in multiple publications worldwide. He currently lives in beautiful New Brunswick, Canada, with his wife, son, and more pets than people. When he is not dipping cookies in a cup of tea or staring at blank pieces of paper, he is usually drawing books. One of the books he illustrated is *The Inquisitor's Tale* by Adam Gidwitz, which won a Newbery Honor and other awards, despite Hatem's drawings of a farting dragon, a two-headed cat, and stinky cheese.